Max
Gets Ready

Fay Robinson
Illustrated by Amelia Rosato

RIGBY

Max can put on his jumper.

Max can put on his trousers.

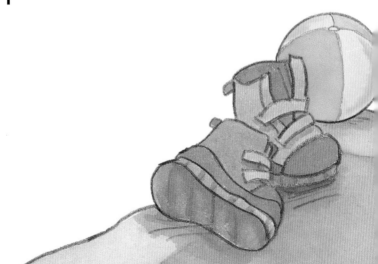

Max can put on his boots.

Max can put on his coat.

Max can put on his hat.

Max can put on his scarf.

Max can put on his mittens.

Help! Max can't move!